Allison Tzu-Yu Lin

London Poetics

· Acknowledgements ·

The initial idea of writing this book comes from Prof Mark Ford's talk in Literary London Conference, 2014. The purpose of writing this book is to encourage colleagues, students and those who are interested in poetry and London, to keep studying and doing research and teaching on the subject.

I would like to thank Mr Michael Song, the President of Showwe Publisher in Taipei. Without his friendship and encouragement, I won't be able to finish writing in a smooth way. I also want to thank Ms Irene Cheng and Mr Jonathan Hung, for all suggestions in the process of publishing this book.

I particularly want to thank my colleagues, students and friends in the Faculty of Education, Gaziantep University. Apart from developing academic interests, they also help me to know myself more, in many priceless conversations and talks.

The last but not the least, I thank my beloved family members, for their understanding and love.

A. L.

Gaziantep 2016

· Preface ·

Professor Mark Ford

The poetry of London is a rich and complex subject and Allison Lin has written an entertaining and wide-ranging account of the many poems that this great city has inspired. This book will prove valuable to all those interested in the history of London and in the history of English poetry. It covers the work of many centuries and many poets. She provides superb examples of the greatest poems written about London, from John Keats to Wendy Cope, from Tennyson to T.S. Eliot. Her commentary on these poems is judicious, perceptive, and assured. So climb aboard this open-topped, double-decker poetic bus, and prepare to enjoy the history of London in verse!

Mark Ford

· Content ·

· Chapter 1 ·

Love

In this chapter, I read several literary texts, in order to demonstrate the relation between the viewing subject and the gazed object, in terms of love, illusion and and aesthetic ecstasy. Walter Benjamin's untitled poem illuminates love and blessing through artistic images, as in Giorgio de Chirico's painting, *The Song of Love* (1914). Love in London is somehow a dream-like image – a surreal illusion of love, which stays in the viewer's mind as a poem of colours, representing eternity. Virginia Woolf's *Night and Day* says it better, when Mary walks into the British Museum and gazes at the Elgin Marbles, thinking how much she is in love with Ralph. John Keats' 'On Seeing the Elgin Marbles' also depicts the way in which a gaze of love could be an eternal moment of aesthetic ecstasy. Finally,

Wendy Cope's two London poems, 'Lonely Hearts' and 'After the Lunch', come to express how love is romantic, in a way which imagination, desire, and even disappointment can be a sentimental experience.

Introduction

Love can be defined in various terms, in different conditions and contexts. When one is alone, love can be seen as a desire. To be alone with one's self somehow is a perfect way to possess the loved object, as one can manipulate the love relation within one's own mind, as the reader can see in Walter Benjamin's note-like poem. In London, Virginia Woolf's character Mary, in *Night and Day*, has her love secret unfolded when seeing the Elgin marbles in the British Museum. Through the gaze, Mary constructs a surreal situation, which goes beyond her present space and time, imaging Ralph as her guardian, who is able to love her in return. The same work of art, when in Keats' poem, the reader can see that the whole experience of gazing at the Elgin marbles turns to be a sense of sympathizing love, for the mortality of one's own physical being, and the limitation of its relation with the others.

Love in Imagination

Let's begin with a poem by Walter Benjamin:

> When I begin a song
> It sticks
> And if I become aware of you
> It is an illusion
>
> And thus love wanted you
> Humble and small
> So that I win you
> With being alone

3

Therefore you slipped from me
Until I learnt
Only flawless petitions

Betray nature
And only enraptured steps
The eternal trace.
    blessed
    (Marx 67)

I am fascinated by this little note-like poem, not only because of its neatness in the use of words, but also the richness of its meanings. The narrator sings a song to a lover, knowing that this feeling of love creates an image of the lover in the narrator's mind. Since the narrator cannot physically be with his or her lover, the narrator comes to focus on seeing the image of the lover, as if he or she 'win[s]' the lover, by even only thinking about that person. However, the lover's image is very much unstable. It is only a changeable illusion, existing in the narrator's mind, which does not have a certain form. It is always slipping away. The narrator has to trace the illusion of the lover, as it is '[b]etray nature' to be in love with someone like this. For the narrator, to have the illusion of being in love is as real as eternity – it is even 'blessed'.

In Giorgio de Chirico's painting, *The Song of Love* (1914), he depicts exactly such a surreal illusion of love, which stays in the viewer's mind as a poem of colours, representing eternity. As in a dream-like illusion, each visual object is not directly connected to another, as if they were picked up randomly: the little white cloud is hanging on the blue sky; on the wall of the building, there are a big head sculpture and a leather glove. The green ball stopped moving. Each visual object has a ridiculous size, which cannot be measured by real terms. All of the visual objects exist in the same space of time, and it looks like they will be there forever. It does not matter which one comes first, to create and to compose the song of love.

Impossible Love

Love is a feeling as real as eternity, as one can see in Benjamin's poem. Love can also be as painful and unbearable, as a physical movement or a practice, as in one's 'soulless travels' (Ford 626) on the road:

A202

This coarse road, my road, struggles out
South-east across London, an exhausted
Grey zigzag of stubborn, unassimilable
  Macadam, passing hoardings pasted

With blow-ups of cricket journalists, blackened
And not-quite-Georgian terraces,

Shagged-out Greens of Geraniums and
  Floral coats-of-arms, lost pieces

Of genteel façade behind and above
Lyons' shopfronts and "Pullum Promotions,"
-Journeying between wired-off bombed lots glossy
  With parked Consuls, making diversions

Round bus depots and draggled estates
In circumlocutory One-Ways,
Netting aquaria in crammed pet store windows,
  Skirting multi-racial bingo queues,

And acquiring, for its self-hating hoard, old black-railed
Underground bogs advising the Seamen's Hospital,
"Do-it-yourself" shops, "Funerals and Monuments," and
  Victorian Charrington pubs. All

Along its length it despoils, in turn, a sequence
Of echoless names: Camberwell, Peckham,
New Cross Gate; places having no recorded past
  Except in histories of the tram.

It takes out, in cars, arterial affluence
At week-ends, returning it as bad blood
To Monday mornings in town. It is altogether
  Like a vein travelled by hardy diseases, an aged

Canal dredgeable for bodies left behind
On its soulless travels; Sixty-Nine,
Thirty-Six, One-Eight-Five. It takes no clear
  Attitude anyone could easily define

So as to resist or admire it. It seems to hate you
Possessively, want to envelop you in nothing
Distinguishable or distinguished, like its own
  Smothered slopes and rotting

Valleys. This road, generally, is one for
The long-defeated; and turns any ironic
Observer's tracer-isotope of ecology,
  Sociology, or hopeful manic

Verse into a kind of mere
Nosing virus itself. It leaves its despondent, foul
And intractable deposit on its own
  Banks all the way like virtually all

Large rivers, particularly the holy ones, which it
Is not. It sees little that deserves to be undespised.
It only means well in the worst of ways.
  How much of love is much less compromised?

(Ford 625-26)

As Alan Brownjohn's narrator asks in the poem, 'A 202', 'How much of love is much less compromised', as one keeps seeing

and enduring the very 'coarse road' (Ford 625-26) across South-
east London. This road, A202, as changeless as an 'exhausted
Grey zigzag of stubborn' (Ford 625), belongs to the traveler
himself. The road itself, even it looks like as if 'soulless' (Ford
626) as it could be, is having 'no clear attitude' toward the
traveler, because the traveler's mood is a complex, specifically
on 'Monday mornings in town' (Ford 625).

In Virginia Woolf's novel *Night and Day*, Mary is depicted
as a character, who turns aesthetic works of art into an imaginary
love relation with Ralph, through her gaze at the Elgin marbles
in the British Museum. Mary's gaze seems to empower the
works of art, as they externalise her 'some wave of exaltation
and emotion' (Woolf 65). Works of art, in Woolf's novel, do
not express something 'purely aesthetic' (Woolf 65), as they are
externalisation of a character through artistic 'shapes'. Mary's

> emotion were not purely aesthetic, because, after
> she had gazed at the Ulysses for a minute or two,
> she began to think about Ralph Denham. So secure

did she feel with these silent shapes that she almost
yielded to an impulse to say 'I am in love with
you' aloud. The presence of this immense and
enduring beauty made her almost alarmingly
conscious of her desire, and at the same time proud
of a feeling which did not display anything like the
same proportions when she was going about her

daily work (Woolf 65-66).

Through Mary, Woolf's writing comes to show that the idea of
Beauty is indeed, an impression of one' own emotion. Mary's
emotion does not reveal the aesthetic value of a work of art. Her
way of seeing does not concern how beautiful the work of art
is, or, its artistic techniques. Mary's emotion of love illuminates
C. Lewis Hind's aesthetic theory. When Hind saw the Assyrian
Winged Bulls, he noticed not the work of art itself, but his own
feelings – that 'something more', both 'strange and stimulating',
transforming 'mere technique into mysticism' (Hind 88-91).
Mary's visual experience in the British Museum particularly

depicts her 'aesthetic ecstasy' (Bell 37), coming to show her realization of her desire and her love. Her way of seeing is a very personal, as if the winged Assyrian bulls and the Elgin Marbles would take her to an epic journey of love.

Here is John Keats' poetic expression of aesthetic emotions, focusing on the Elgin Marbles:

On seeing the Elgin Marbles

My spirit is too weak – mortality
  Weights heavily on me like unwilling sleep;
  And each imagined pinnacle and steep
Of godlike hardship tells me I must die
Like a sick eagle looking at the sky.
  Yet 'tis a gentle luxury to weep
  That I have not the cloudy winds to keep
Fresh for the opening of the morning's eye.
Such dim-conceivèd glories of the brain
  Bring round the heart an undescribable feud:

So do these wonders a most dizzy pain,

   That mingles Grecian grandeur with the rude

Wasting of old Time, with a billowy main,

   A sun, a shadow of a magnitude.

(Ford 364)

According to Clarke Olney, Keats' 'On Seeing the Elgin Marbles'

> were the immediate results of a visit to the
> British Museum under Haydon's guidance. On
> this visit, if one may trust Haydon's later
> recollection, the two enthusiasts were
> accompanied by John Hamilton Reynolds. The
> marbles made a profound impression upon
> Keats, and with Haydon as his guide it is little
> wonder, for he, better perhaps than any man in
> London, loved the marbles and had mastered
> their meaning (Olney 262).

Between 1817 and 1818, John Keats and the painter Benjamin Robert Haydon began their 'intimate friendship' (Olney 260), which had a great impact on Keats' poetry. 'Haydon was thirty-one, Keats ten years his junior: both were young and passionately intense in their love for beauty' (Olney 261). Both the young artist's and the young poet's (Keats was 'virtually unknown') love for artistic creation makes them think about each other as 'truly one of those, / Whose sense discerns the loveliness of things' (qtd. in Olney, 260).

Haydon believes that art should be the 'powerful', the 'grand', in order to achieve the 'highest', the 'most "sublime" themes' (Olney 274). This aesthetic ideology somehow does not necessarily represent Keats' own poetic senses, as his 'On Seeing the Elgin Marbles' would show. Although 'sorrow' and 'hopeless love' (Olney 275) in Keats' poem are not exactly the emotions that Haydon needs, for his grand 'historical or religious themes' (Olney 275), the intense friendship between two artists somehow becomes immortal, as Beauty and the intense aesthetic emotions the viewer's – which is 'a gentle luxury' to cry (Ford 364).

Romantic Love

Wendy Cope's two poems, 'Lonely Hearts' and 'After the Lunch', come to express a condition, in which love is a kind of romantic hope. Because of being romantic, even disappointment, even the unknown, feels romantic.

Lonely Hearts

Can someone make my simple wish come true?
Male biker seeks female for touring fun.
Do you live in North London? Is it you?

Gay vegetarian whose friends are few,
I'm into music, Shakespeare and the sun.
Can someone make my simple wish come true?

Executive in search of something new –
Perhaps bisexual woman, arty, young.
Do you live in North London? Is it you?

Successful, straight and solvent? I am too –
Attractive Jewish lady with a son.
Can someone make my simple wish come true?

I'm Libran, inexperienced and blue –
Need slim non-smoker, under twenty-one.
Do you live in North London? Is it you?

Please write (with photo) to Box 152.
Who knows where it may lead once we've begun?
Can someone make my simple wish come true?
Do you live in North London? Is it you? (Ford 666)

In this poem, the reader can see that all different kinds of
people are having the same wish – to be in love (either to be

loved, or, to love) – although they all have different kinds of wish-image in their minds. A male biker is looking for a female, to ride the bike together and to have fun. A gay vegetarian, who loves Shakespeare, music and the sun, is looking for a lover, and praying for having his wish come true.

But all these people happen to live in North London – a bisexual woman, 'arty' and 'young', an '[a]ttractive Jewish lady with a son' – who is 'successful', 'straight' and 'solvent' (Ford 666). A person whose star sign is Libra, not very experienced in love or in relationships, has a very specific request – he or she (most probably 'he') needs 'slim non-smoker, under twenty-one' (Ford 666).

Although the meaning of love is not easy to define at all, somehow, it can start with something visual, as the narrator requests – '[p]lease write (with photo) to Box 152'. A photo may not represent something as love at first sight, still, it is a good way to identify a possible chemical reaction, if there is, when in love.

After the Lunch

On Waterloo Bridge, where we said our goodbyes,
The weather conditions bring tears to my eyes.
I wipe them away with a black woolly glove
And try not to notice I've fallen in love.

On Waterloo Bridge I am trying to think:
This is nothing. You're high on the charm and the drink.
But the juke-box inside me is playing a song
That says something different. And when was it wrong?

On Waterloo Bridge with the wind in my hair
I am tempted to skip. *You're a fool.* I don't care.
The head does its best but the heart is the boss –
I admit it before I am halfway across. (Ford 667)

After the lunch, on Waterloo Bridge, the lovers said 'goodbyes', but not as a casual 'see you later' sense. They are separating from each other, saying goodbye to this love relationship. 'The weather conditions' are windy ('with wind in my hair', Ford 667) and rainy, as the narrator has tears in the eyes (probably mixed with rain). The narrator 'I' wipe the tears, as a gesture of trying to cover his or her falling out of love.

The narrator is trying to 'think' (Ford 667) – trying to make sense and to be reasonable, in order to analyse when and what went wrong in the love relationship. The 'juke-box inside' (Ford 667) the narrator can be representing the narrator's heart. While trying to think about the whole thing with the organ of reason, the brain; the organ of emotion, the heart, is suggesting something else, which cannot be figured out with reason. Although the narrator seems to get hurt by ending this love, calling him/herself '*a fool*', he or she admits it - loving so much like a fool, before 'halfway across' the bridge.

Conclusion

Through literary texts, the reader is able to identify words which represent feelings of love. An understanding of love is difficult to achieve, as there is no one single way to define love. Words and images are in the same complex, trying to express the moment of eternity that one feels in love. As one gazes at the work of art, somehow imagination and feeling come together, synthesizing the meaning of love, as a part of experiences in life.

Works Cited

Bell, Clive. *Art.* London: Chatto and Windus, 1947.

Ford, Mark, ed. *London: A History in Verse.* Cambridge, MA: Harvard University Press, 2012.

Hind, C. Lewis. *The Post-Impressionists.* London: Methuen, 1911.

Marx, Ursula, et al, eds. *Walter Benjamin's Archive:Images, Texts, Signs.* Trans. Esther Leslie. London: Verso, 2007.

Olney, Clarke. 'John Keats and Benjamin Robert Haydon'. *PMLA* 49.1 (1934), 258-275.

Woolf, Virginia. *Night and Day.* Ed. Julia Briggs. London: Penguin, 1992.

London Poetics

· Chapter 2 ·

History

In this chapter, I read different poems of London through the perspectives of time and the self. The city of London, as a physical space, a world in the globe, is changing through both inner time and outer time. Firstly, in Lord Alfred Tennyson's *Cleopatra's Needle*, the flow of tide symbolises the passing time, through the long Egyptian history to Tennyson's Victorian London. The Needle has been through different seas and places. The sense of history, a fusion of inner time and outer time, is claimed by the Needle's subjective self, seeing London as a 'monster town'. Secondly, Ahren Warner's Greek titled poem is trying to locate the one in London, which cannot be localized, in the trend of globalization, as the gazer observed on the bus. Struggling between the self and the other, inner and outer existences, happiness and being unhappy, W B Yeats' from *Vacillation* comes to show the reader that through reflection and memory, the sense of one's own self can be reinforced and affirmed, while creating one's own personal history. The last but not the least, I read a part from T. S. Eliot's *Four Quartets*. As the dialectic of light and shadow plays a sense of Beauty, the soul is aware of all fancy things, but only without any meanings. The question of the self and tradition, the poet and the world, somehow, is a timeless one.

Introduction

It does not come easy at all, when one tries to define what history is. Sometime it becomes more difficult, when one tries further, to re-discover the meaning of history. Although my initial aim of reading these London poems was to find out something else, magically, the definition of History in these poems somehow come together as quite a self-fulfillment.

History, in these London poems I chose to read, can be seen as small as a personal event – as Yeats' own birthday reflection and memory, in a way which is totally self-centered and is referring to a completely personal experience. And yet, in these London poems, the readers can see that anything big, such as tradition, time, or the term History with a capitalised 'H', must come from something as small as one's own self. The definition of the term History can be varied. As in Tennyson's poem, *Cleopatra's Needle*, the Needle sees the ups and the downs of the empires. The memory comes to the viewing subject, while standing by the River Thames. The fusion of the past and the present comes, as the Needle concludes to himself – 'I was when London was not. / I am here' (Ford 387).

The history of globalization can be seen in London, when the viewing subject is trying to define, or, to be more precise, to localise the happy outsider in Ahren Warner's poem. History comes to a point, when people come together on the London bus, and go to their own different destinations. History seems to be a joint fate, when in London. It does not matter one is happy or not. In my reading of Eliot's London poem, I somehow feel that the emptiness and the meaningless of the self and of History can be regained through an embracement of tradition and intellectual labour, as Eliot himself implied in his essay.

Subject, Object, and History

Cleopatra's Needle
Here, I that stood in On beside the flow
Of sacred Nile, three thousand years ago! –
A Pharaoh, kingliest of his kingly race,
First shaped, and carved, and set me in my place.
A Caesar of a punier dynasty
Thence haled me toward the Mediterranean sea,
Whence your own citizens, for their own renown,
Through strange seas drew me to your monster town.
I have seen the four great empires disappear.
I was when London was not. I am here (Ford 387).

In Alfred, Lord Tennyson's *Cleopatra's Needle*, the sense of history is extremely strong. In the past, Cleopatra's Needle 'stood in On beside the flow / Of sacred Nile'. But now (including Tennyson's and our presents), Cleopatra's Needle is standing 'beside the flow' of the Thames River in London. In between, there is at least a time difference of 'three thousand years'. During these years, the subjective 'I' of Cleopatra's Needle had travelled and had moved among the seas. Through the changing tide of different seas, history is created in the form of 'four great empires', explaining the way in which the Needle was built, and who put it in the place. Now the Needle is in London – a place which is addressed as a 'monster town', where everything is possible, especially 'darkness' (Agathocleous 185) as in Charles Dickens's novels. And yet, the Needle's existence expresses something beyond the measurement of time, simply as one can see in the subjective claim of Cleopatra's Needle, 'when London was not, I am here'.

For a global city like London, it is really difficult to say

27

what is local and what is not, with all kinds of people, culture and things coming to exist together, in the same place, and yet passing through different time. In Cleopatra's Needle's eye, the 'I' certainly define London as a 'monster town' – big, strange, not necessarily beautiful. However, in Ahren Warner's Greek titled poem, the reader can also see again, this kind of time and space complicity and confusion:

Girl with ridiculous earrings   why do you bother
to slap the boy   we all assume is your boyfriend
and is lolling over   that bus seat   shouting

it's a London thing.   He is obviously a knob
but a happy one   and that   it seems to me
is the important   though not localisable   thing (Ford 726).

Many elements mentioned in the poem are 'not localisable', for many reasons. For instance, why the girl's earrings are 'ridiculous' – compare to what (other objects), to where (other cities and places), to whom (everyone else, or someone specific), to when (her present time, or some other historical time)? Why the girl even bother to 'slap' the boy, as if 'shouting' in the bus and 'lolling over' the bus seat are totally foreign to Londoners. What if he is not her boyfriend? Can she still slap him? Will the whole thing feel differently? Why it is '*a London thing*'? How can he be 'a knob' and yet very happy? Which one is 'not localisable' – the knob or the happy one?

The sense of history is also in the inner self, as a kind of personal history, reflection and memory. Through reflection and memory, the sense of one's 'self' can be reinforced and affirmed, while creating one's own personal history. W. B. Yeats' poem shows the reader such a significant moment of solitude and reflection.

from *Vacillation*

My fiftieth year had come and gone,
I sat, a solitary man,

In a crowded London shop,
An open book and empty cup
On the marble table-top.
While on the shop and street I gazed
My body of a sudden blazed;
And twenty minutes more or less
It seemed, so great my happiness,
That I was blessed and could bless (Ford 482).

The poet sat in the crowd, in a London coffee shop, reflecting his past fifty years. On the marble coffee table, there are a book and an empty cup. The cup is empty, showing that he has been there for some time, done some reading and drinking. While he looked around, for about twenty minutes, he felt a great joy, as if his body was on fire, burning, feeling happy, and feeling blessed and was able to give bless to other people.

Poet, Tradition, and the Globe

Time is a significant issue, in the city of London. In T. S. Eliot's poem, the relation between time and space comes to show the essence of London, in a way which London is a place 'in a dim light', expressing a feeling of 'lucid stillness'.

T. S. Eliot
from *Four Quartets*
from Burnt Norton
III
Here is a place of disaffection
Time before and time after
In a dim light: neither daylight
Investing form with lucid stillness
Turning shadow into transient beauty
With slow rotation suggesting permanence

Nor darkness to purify the soul

Emptying the sensual with deprivation

Cleansing affection from the temporal.

Neither plentitude nor vacancy. Only a flicker

Over the strained time-ridden faces

Distracted from distraction by distraction

Filled with fancies and empty of meaning

Tumid apathy with no concentration

Men and bits of paper, whirled by the cold wind

That blows before and after time,

Wind in and out of unwholesome lungs

Time before and time after.

Eructation of unhealthy souls

Into the faded air, the torpid

Driven on the wind that sweeps the gloomy hills of London.

Hampstead and Clerkenwell, Campden and Putney,

Highgate, Primrose and Ludgate. Not here

Not here the darkness, in this twittering world.

Descend lower, descend only

Into the world of perpetual solitude,

World not world, but that which is not world,

Internal darkness, deprivation

And destitution of all property,

Desiccation of the world of sense,

Evacuation of the world of fancy,

Inoperancy of the world of spirit;

This is the one way, and the other

Is the same, not in movement

But abstention from movement; while the world moves

In appetency, on its metalled ways

Of time past and time future (Ford 517-18).

The dialectic of light and shadow indicates a kind of 'transient beauty'. Somehow the temporal signs are on the poets' faces ('men and bits of paper'). They are faces of 'time-ridden', like souls which 'nor darkness to purify' – profound and complicated. The status of standstill, as something is 'distracted from distraction by distraction / filled with fancies and empty of meaning'. Everything seems to be changing, and yet, to a status of changing same. It does not matter 'time before and time after', or 'time past and time future', the wind 'sweeps the gloomy hills of London / Hampstead and Clerkenwell, Campden and Putney, / Highgate, Primrose and Ludgate'. The centre of the soul is solitude and dark, even if the external world is unsettle and 'twittering'.

Without the self and his or her own identity, history, either personal or non-personal, will be merely like a very dry story – just as an 'empty space' (Eagleton 46), showing an image of 'whorelike' 'emptiness' (Eagleton 45) – as the self and the soul are detached, in T. S. Eliot's poem, from 'the world of sense', 'the world of fancy', and 'the world of spirit' (Ford 517-518). Although human faces are 'time-ridden' (Ford 517), still, those faces only represent something which are 'distracted from distraction by distraction' (Ford 517), totally meaningless, without any sense of cultural root or centre. Everything is up in the air – no order, 'no concentration' (Ford 517) – just like poets and their papers – blowing. As 'the cold wind' (Ford 517) blows in and out of people's lungs, their 'unhealthy souls' (Ford 517) seem to be fading away, together with the sweeping wind that blows 'the gloomy hills of London' – from 'Hampstead and Clerkenwell, Campden and Putney', all the way to 'Highgate, Primrose and Ludgate' (Ford 517).

Through 'a feeling' (Eliot 2320) of having the literary tradition in mind, the poet 'has a simultaneous existence' with 'his own contemporaneity', as 'the historical sense' is somehow a feeling of timelessness, which comes to against the physical movement of the external world – the whole temporal and spatial existence. As Eliot himself stated in his 'Tradition and the Individual Talent', the sense of history is a perception, in a way which the self is in his contemporary, while showing his awareness of the past, the tradition. It is worth it to quote the whole paragraph:

> Yet if the only form of tradition, of handing down, consisted in following the ways of the immediate generation before us in a blind or timid adherence to its

successes, 'tradition' should positively be discouraged. We have seen many such simple currents soon lost in the sand; and novelty is better than repetition. Tradition is a matter of much wider significance. It cannot be inherited, and if you want it you must obtain it by great labour. It involves, in the first place, the historical sense, which we may call nearly indispensable to any one who would continue to be a poet beyond his twenty-fifth year; and the historical sense involves a perception, not only of the pastness of the past, but of its presence; the historical sense compels a man to write not merely with his own generation in his bones, but with a feeling that the whole of the literature of Europe from Homer and within it the whole of the literature of his own country has a simultaneous existence and composes a simultaneous order. This historical sense, which is a sense of timeless as well as of the temporal and of the timeless and of the temporal together, is what makes a writer traditional. And it is at the same time what makes a writer most

acutely conscious of his place in time, of his own
contemporaneity
(Eliot 2320).

Again, in this paragraph, one can see many binary oppositions
coming together as dialectics, as in Eliot's poem – such as
timeless verses the temporal, tradition verses contemporaneity.
A poet's historical sense means not only a 'perception', but also
'a feeling that the whole of the literature of Europe from Homer
and within it the whole of the literature of his own country has
a simultaneous existence and composes a simultaneous order'
(Eliot 2320). And yet, a poet, together with the tradition (the
whole literature of Europe and his own country), there is a
'contemporaneity' can be formed, and to be called, as his own.
This literature of one's own does not come easy at all. A poet
needs to work hard to read through the tradition, not only in a
sense of its 'pastness', but also with his own perception in his
present, Without doing that, all so-called 'new' ideas would be
like 'simple currents', worthless and easy to fade away.

Without tradition, the self and anything which can be called 'new', is easy to be 'lost in the sand' (Eliot 2320). As the wave of time comes, if there is no centre, no tradition, no identity, no root to hold on to, the so-called 'present' will not be meaningful. I would suggest that in Eliot's poem, all will be representing nothing but a 'whorelike' 'emptiness' (Eagleton 45), because this feeling of emptiness and meaningless comes from a humanity, which is in pain for all kinds of reasons: war, poverty, psychological disorder, and so on, and so forth, as Brunet feels and sees in Jean-Paul Sartre's *Iron in the Soul*, 'a machine-gun' has twisted the world, made his head empty, for the very reason that humanity is suffering – 'Suffering humanity - [...] like dogs!' (Sartre 256).

This kind of humanity, in pain, suffering, could be one of the most shocking awareness of 'contemporary emptiness', as Frank Lentricchia once phrased it in his *Modernist Quartet* (Lentricchia 246). The feeling of emptiness can be read as a situation of being lost, as human faces are 'time-ridden', 'Distracted from distraction by distraction / Filled with fancies and empty of meaning' (Ford 517). And yet, the feeling of emptiness can also be read as a sign, in a way which the self somehow loses his or her contact with tradition, as the concept of tradition can be interpreted as the representation of history and cultural heritage. Without a literary and a historical point of view, the self will not be able to 'remake history on his own terms' (Bann 103). In other words, the self will need to remake tradition, so that it can be of his own.

Conclusion

The meaning of life, in London, somehow is a representation of a unity. The dialectic of the opposite poles, such as emptiness and hope, memory and the present, local and the 'not localisable', 'time before and time after' – becomes a kind of realization of humanity. Instead of merely looking at 'une passante' in a poetic sense of Baudelaire's, as if taking snapshots of each present moment, the London selves are doing something different. The London poems I read in this research show the readers the importance of thinking: either remembering of one's own past, or obtaining the tradition to the contemporary self, or thinking about Londoners in a global context, or looking at the city and being aware of one's own existence – in reading some aspects of London poems, one can start to be sure that 'only a redeemed mankind receives the fullness of its past – which is to say, only for a redeemed mankind has its past become citable in all its moments' (Benjamin 254). The self, and his or her own memory and reflection, are not historically determined or labelled. They are, on the contrary, in a process of writing a history, of London and the globe.

Works Cited

Agathocleous, Tanya. *Urban Realism and the Cosmopolitan Imagination in the Nineteenth Century: Visible City,*

InvisibleWorld. Cambridge: Cambridge University Press, 2011.

Bann, Stephen. 'The Sense of the Past: Image, Text, and Object in the Formation of Historical Consciousness in Nineteenth-Century Britain'. Veeser 102 – 115.

Benjamin, Walter. *Illuminations: Essays and Reflections.* Trans. Harry Zohn. New York: Schocken, 1968.

Ford, Mark, ed. *London: A History in Verse.* Cambridge, MA: Harvard University Press, 2012.

Eagleton, Terry. *Walter Benjamin or Towards a Revolutionary Criticism.* London: Verso, 1994.

Eliot, T. S. 'Tradition and the Individual Talent'. *The Norton Anthology of English Literature: Volume 2.* Eds. Stephen Greenblatt and M. H. Abrams. New York: W. W. Norton, 2006.

Lentricchia, Frank. *Modernist Quartet.* Cambridge: Cambridge UP, 1994.

Sartre, Jean-Paul. *Iron in the Soul.* Trans. Gerard Hopkins. Middlesex: Penguin, 1963.

Veeser, H. Aram, ed. *The New Historicism.* London: Routledge, 1989.

· Chapter 3 ·

Metropolis

In this chapter, we will read the city of London in its somatic parts, in its movement and its motions. Different parts of London are linked by sensual experiences, such as the gaze, the small, the talk, the sound – some of them are in the public space, some are in the private space. Through the gaze, the body parts of London somehow come to represent an inner space, as the psychology of the viewers is reflected on what they see. Three poems will be read: Thomas Jordan's 'from *The Triumphs of London*', George Eliot's 'In a London Drawingroom', Richard Aldington's 'In the Tube', Seamus Heaney's *The Underground*.

Thomas Jordan
from *The Triumphs of London*

You that delight in wit and mirth,
  And love to hear such news
As comes from all parts of the earth,
  Dutch, Danes, and Turks, and Jews;
I'll send ye to a rendezvous,
  Where it is smoking new;
Go hear it at a Coffee-house,
  It cannot but be true.

There battles are sea-fights are fought,
  And bloody plots displayed;
They know more things than e'er was thought,
  Or ever was betrayed:
No money in the Minting-house,

Is half so bright and new;
And coming from a Coffee-house,
  It cannot but be true.

Before the navies fell to work,
  They knew who should be winner;
They there can tell ye what the Turk
  Last Sunday had to dinner.
Who last did cut De Ruyter's corns,
  Amongst his jovial crew;
Or who first gave the devil horns,
  Which cannot but be true.

A fisherman did boldly tell,
  And strongly did avouch,
He caught a shoal of mackerel,
  They parleyed all in Dutch;
And cried out *Yaw, yaw, yaw, mine here,*

And as the draught they drew,
They shook for fear that Monk was there –
   This sounds as if 'twere true.

There is nothing done in all the world,
   From monarch to the mouse,
But every day or night 'tis hurled
   Into the Coffee-house:
What Lilly or what Booker could
   By art not bring about,
At Coffee-house you'll find a brood
   Can quickly find it out.

They know who shall in times to come
   Be either made or undone;
From great St. Peter's Street in Rome
   To Turnbull Street in London.
And likewise tell at Clerkenwell,

What whore hath greatest gain;
And in that place what brazen face
    Doth wear a golden chain.

They know all that is good or hurt,
    To damn ye or to save ye;
There is the college and the court,
    The country, camp, and navy.
So great an university,
    I think there ne'er was any,
In which you may a scholar be,
    For spending of a penny.

Here men do talk of everything,
    With large and liberal lungs,
Like women at a gossiping,
    With double tire of tongues;
They'll give a broadside presently,

'Soon as you are in view,
With stories that you'll wonder at,
   Which they will swear are true.

You shall know there what fashions are,
   How perriwigs are curled;
And for a penny you shall hear
   All novels in the world;
Both old and young, and great and small,
   And rich and poor you'll see;
Therefore let's to the coffee all,
   Come all away with me (Ford 162 – 164).

In this poem, the city of London is depicted as a miniature of the world through different kinds of sensual experiences – namely, hearing people's talk (wit, delightful), stories and gossips, looking at the latest fashion (the curly wig, the golden chain), people's faces in the view. All these sensual experiences come from all kinds of people, including Dutch, Danes (the various

Viking tribes), Turks and Jews. The Coffee-house represents
an impression of London, with all kinds of social classes –
representing by a fisherman, a whore (prostitute), monarch and a
mouse. The stories, novels and gossips seem to make the Coffee-
house a university, as if everyone in it is a scholar, talking 'with
large and liberal lung' (very loud voices, full of energy).

Although the Coffee-house is not an open space, the next
poem will show us what a poet can do, in a very different way,
comes to depict quite an opposite atmosphere in an interior.

George Eliot
In a London Drawingroom

The sky is cloudy, yellowed by the smoke.
For view there are the houses opposite
Cutting the sky with one long line of wall
Like the solid fog: far as the eye can stretch
Monotony of surface & of the form

Without a break to hang a guess upon.
No bird can make a shadow as it flies,
For all its shadow, as in ways o'erhung
By thickest canvas, where the golden rays
Are clothed in hemp. No figure lingering
Pauses to feed the hunger of the eye
Or rest a little on the lap of life.
All hurry on & look upon the ground,
Or glance unmarking at the passers by.
The wheels are hurrying too, cabs, carriages
All closed, in multiplied identity.
The world seems one huge prison-house & court
Where men are punished at the slightest cost,
With lowest rate of colour, warmth & joy (Ford 402).

In this poem, life itself, at least life in London, is not very much colourful and enjoyable. Everything one sees is 'with lowest rate of colour, warmth & joy', as the world of London is 'one huge prison-house'. In *The Triumph of London*, in the Coffee-house, the city itself is to be taken as the world itself. And yet, *In a London Drawingroom* comes to show everything in an opposite way: 'the sky is cloudy', and things are not to be seen clearly, because of the industrial smoke (as one can see in the film, *Mr Turner*). In *The Triumph of London*, everything is 'smoking new' – burning, hot, exciting, with the talk of smokers in the Coffeehouse.

Only the view of the houses can be seen, slightly clearer, 'cutting the sky with one long line of the wall'. But even the sky cannot create a feeling of being free, as 'no bird can make a shadow as it flies'. The sky is so cloudy, like a very thick canvas, in which the sun ('the golden rays') cannot penetrate. 'The eye' keeps observing, from a London drawingroom, looking outside. The street of London is full of people who are in a hurry, and are looking upon the ground. Some people are looking at 'the passers by', without any specific purposes ('glance unmarking'), or without any specific feelings or senses.

The whole city seems to be very busy, even the traffic ('the wheels') are 'hurrying too'. All kinds of transportation forms –

cabs, carriages, are closed (cannot see the inside). Everyone is busy with their own business, 'in multiple identity', but without any feeling of joy, warmth, or the vibratility of colour.(as one can see in Van Gogh's painting).

Richard Aldington
In the Tube

The electric car jerks;
I stumble on the slats of the floor,
Fall into a leather seat
And look up.

A row of advertisements,
A row of windows,
Set in brown woodwork pitted with brass nails,
A row of hard faces,
Immobile,

In the swaying train,

Rush across the flickering background of fluted dingy tunnel;

A row of eyes,

Eyes of greed, of pitiful blankness, of plethoric complacency,

Immobile,

Gaze, stare at one point,

At my eyes.

Antagonism,

Disgust,

Immdediate antipathy,

Cut my brain, as a dry sharp reed

Cuts a finger.

I surprise the same thought

In the brasslike eyes:

"*What right have you to live?*" (Ford 521)

    The narrator gets into the 'electric car' of the underground, sitting down in 'a leather seat'. At the moment when the narrator sits down, this person observes the environment he is situated in – 'a row of advertisements', 'a row of windows', 'a row of hard faces' (people who are also sitting in the electric car).

The train moves fast in the tunnel. But people can only sit, not moving ('immobile'). The narrator also sees 'A row of eyes, / Eyes of greed, of pitiful blankness, of plethoric complacency'. These people gaze at the narrator, arousing different kinds of emotions inside him – 'antagonism', 'disgust', 'immediate antipathy'. These emotions are so sharp, coming to cut his brain ('as a dry sharp reed'), to cut his body into parts ('cuts a finger'). At the same moment, it seems that the Gaze and the consciousness come into one, through the tunnel, as the public sphere (the electric car) and private sphere (the thought) are linked through the Gaze. Those people, somehow shamelessly, are thinking what he is thinking – *"What right have you to live?"*

Seamus Heaney
The Underground

There we were in the vaulted tunnel running,
You in your going-away coat speeding ahead
And me, me then like a fleet god gaining
Upon you before you turned to a reed

Or some new white flower japed with crimson
As the coat flapped wild and button after button
Sprang off and fell in a trail
Between the Underground and the Albert Hall.

Honeymooning, moonlighting, late for the Proms,
Our echoes die in that corridor and now
I come as Hansel came on the moonlit stones
Retracing the path back, lifting the buttons

To end up in a draughty lamplit station
After the trains have gone, the wet track
Bared and tensed as I am, all attention
For your step following and damned if I look back (Ford 646).

Gaze, feeling, motion – these are the key ideas of both poems, *In the Tube* and *Underground*. In the poem *Underground,* in the tunnel, again we have characters (but only focusing on two people this time) – 'you', and 'I', come to 'we'. The gaze in this poem is both emotional and physical (we were running). 'You' and 'I' are the fundamental elements of Heaney's flow of images. The reed, instead of referring to something sharp (as in the poem *In the Tube* shows), it is the reference for the Greek mythology, Pan's pursuit of Syrinx, who turned into a reed (Ovid's Metamorphoses).

The flow of images in the poem *Underground* reveals the way in which the gaze and the sound ('our echoes') come together, showing emotions. 'You' and 'I' are chasing each other, as the coat flapped and the buttons dropping, as they are late for the Prom – the BBC music concert (in August and in September each year) at the Royal Albert Hall, near South Kensington Underground Station, in London.

The 'I', like Hansel in the story 'Hansel and Gretel' by the Grimm Brothers, try to follow 'the moonlit stones' to get home. But in the Underground, the 'I', instead of following the moonlit stones, come to follow the 'buttons' of the coat (of 'You'). The station is quiet, 'after the train is gone'. But the 'I' is listening to the steps (hopefully from 'You'), creating a sense of emotional intensity, with 'all attention', as if the eyes are closed, and 'I' would not dare enough to look back.

*Questions for discussions and further studies:

1.Go to The National Gallery website, to see the painting *Pan and Syrinx*: http://www.nationalgallery.org.uk/paintings/ francois-boucher-pan-and-syrinx (François Boucher, 1759). Listen to Louise Govier's talk on the eroticism in the painting.

There are many different versions of visual interpretations of this mythological theme. See also http://www.getty.edu/art/ collection/objects/732/jean-francois-de-troy-pan-and-syrinx- french-1722-1724/ for another painterly expression by Jean- François de Troy (French, 1679 - 1752).

2.Read Seamus Heaney's *District and Circle*, analyse sensual experiences in the poem.

District and Circle

Tunes from a tin whistle underground
Curled up a corridor I'd be walking down
To where I knew I was always going to find
My watcher on the tiles, cap by his side,
His fingers perked, his two eyes eyeing me
In an unaccusing look I'd not avoid,
Or not just yet, since both were out to see

For ourselves.

       As the music larked and capered

I'd trigger and untrigger a hot coin

Held at the ready, but now my gaze was lowered

For was our traffic not in recognition?

Accorded passage, I would re-pocket and nod,

And he, still eyeing me, would also nod.

*

Posted, eyes front, along the dreamy ramparts

Of escalators ascending and descending

To a monotonous slight rocking in the works,

We were moved along, upstanding.

Elsewhere, underneath, an engine powered,

Rumbled, quickened, evened, quieted.

The white tiles gleamed. In passages that flowed

With draughts from cooler tunnels, I missed the light

Of all-overing, long since mysterious day,

Parks at lunchtime where the sunners lay

On body-heated mown grass regardless,

A resurrection, habitués
Of their garden of delights, of staggered summer.
*

Another level down, the platform thronged.
I re-entered the safety of numbers,
A crowd half straggle-ravelled and half strung
Like a human chain, the pushy newcomers
Jostling and purling underneath the vault,
On their marks to be first through the doors,
Street-loud, then succumbing to herd-quiet . . .
Had I betrayed or not, myself or him?
Always new to me, always familiar,
This unrepentant, now repentant turn
As I stood waiting, glad of a first tremor,
Then caught up in the now-or-never whelm
Of one and all the full length of the train.
*

Stepping on to it across the gap,
On to the carriage metal, I reached to grab

The stubby black roof-wort and take my stand
From planted ball of heel to heel of hand
As sweet traction and heavy down-slump stayed me.
I was on my way, well girded, yet on edge,
Spot-rooted, buoyed, aloof,
Listening to the dwindling noises off,
My back to the unclosed door, the platform empty;
And wished it could have lasted,
That long between-times pause before the budge
And glaze-over, when any forwardness
Was unwelcome and bodies readjusted,
Blindsided to themselves and other bodies.
*

So deeper into it, crowd-swept, strap-hanging,
My lofted arm a-swivel like a flail,
My father's glazed face in my own waning
And craning . . .
                    Again the growl
Of shutting doors, the jolt and one-off treble

Of iron on iron, then a long centrifugal
Haulage of speed through every dragging socket.
And so by night and day to be transported
Through galleried earth with them, the only relict
Of all that I belonged to, hurtled forward,
Reflecting in a window mirror-backed
By blasted weeping rock-walls.

Flicker-lit. (Ford 649)

· Chapter 4 ·

Teaching London Poetry and Cultural Exchange

This research aims to answer this question: how can students learn, identify, and appreciate London poetry? In the process of teaching, can cultural exchange happen? Does it give birth to a new cultural identity through English teaching and learning, focusing on the skills of listening, speaking, reading and writing? Through narrating the self, students can express themselves in writing, to identify their own life experiences in London poems in which they read in the class. Through literacy practices in the class, students can understand not only the meaning of the texts. Rather, they develop a sort of interest in British culture through reading London poetry. After identifying with narrating subjects in the poems, my students explore cultural differences between Turkish and British ones. Through comparing both cultures, my students synthesise these two, in order to develop a new cultural identity of their own.

Introduction

In 'Teaching English and Cultural Exchange in Gaziantep', Allison Lin concluded her book chapter in a very optimistic way, as 'discussions of philosophy, politics, arts and literature help one to use English in different cultures, communicating ideas and beliefs among people' (Lin, 'Teaching English and Cultural Exchange in Gaziantep' 41). In the classroom of teaching English Literature, cultural exchange is possible. London poetry represents writings about London, in a literary form such as a poem. As the capital of Britain and 'the flower of cities all' (Ford 3), London is, indeed, a city of rich literary power, which comes to 'inspire in the poet a sense of the sublime' (Ford 2). With full literary energy and power, poets through different historical periods and backgrounds come to write about London, celebrating the 'quality of awesome' and this 'loftiness of thought and feelings in literature' (Baldick 321). The results, as the reader can see, are 'terrifying impressive' (Baldick 321) when it comes to associate and to appreciate London impressions – London's cityscape and landscape.

And yet, for my students in the Department of Foreign Language Education, Gaziantep University, most of them (both Turkish and International students) have never been to London. The city itself, for my students, is only a name in English books. Now, in the class, they need to read, to understand, and to be able to make comments on poems which are about London. How can it be possible?

Nevertheless, most of my students do not have English problems, particularly in terms of reading and writing. The most important thing, for them, is to understand the English way of expression British culture, in the context of teaching and learning in the class, in Turkey. I, more than once, tell my students that for learning poetry, one must try to read the poem out loud, in order to listen to the sound and to feel the meaning of a poem. A poem is not a novel. It does not have too many descriptions and details of a scene, an emotion, or a thought. That is why it is not suitable to be read quietly, in order to pass a long silent time. When reading it out loud, through the changing of rhymes, images, and sounds of a poem, the reader can somehow feel the words better. When the reader does have feelings to a poem, he or she can apply personal approaches to the interpretation and the understanding of a poem, as the poetic language comes from the poet's / the speaker's personal life experiences.

Tennyson and Empathy

London poetry certainly represents a certain kinds of British culture – in terms of British ways of living, thinking, seeing the city itself and the world. For my students, this is their first time to read anything, particularly poems, about London. In that case, I did not choose something too difficult or too complicated for them, in terms of the vocabulary and the meaning of a poem. Some poems look so simple, so clear on the surface, as pure as water – as water is tasteless, does not smell – one cannot talk about something so simple as water – those poems are just like 'pure poetry', which are something make us 'cry, not to lecture' (Woolf 242). And yet, they do have deep meanings and emotions, as Alfred Lord Tennyson's *In Memoriam*.

Comparing to Tennyson's *Cleopatra's Needle*, my students feel more for *In Memoriam*, because it is a poem which expresses much more personal emotions. Let's read these two poems first.

Cleopatra's Needle

Here, I that stood in On beside the flow
Of sacred Nile, three thousand years ago! –
A Pharaoh, kingliest of his kingly race,
First shaped, and carved, and set me in my place.

A Caesar of a punier dynasty
Thence haled me toward the Mediterranean sea,
Whence your own citizens, for their own renown,
Through strange seas drew me to your monster town.
I have seen the four great empires disappear.
I was when London was not. I am here (Ford 387).

from *In Memoriam*

VII

Dark house, by which once more I stand
  Here in the long unlovely street,
  Doors, where my heart was used to beat
So quickly, waiting for a hand,

A hand that can be clasped no more –
  Behold me, for I cannot sleep,

And like a guilty thing I creep
At earliest morning to the door.

He is not here; but far away
  The noise of life begins again,
  And ghastly through the drizzling rain
On the bald street breaks the blank day (Ford 383).

Interestingly, nearly all my students who studied these two poems, had more feelings toward the one from *In Memoriam*. The 'I' in *Cleopatra's Needle* seems to be a more powerful figure, since the Needle is still in the Embankment in London, by the River Thames. It was created by a Pharaoh, who is the king of the kings, to be a symbol of the power of the empire. Even so, the Needle has been moved from one place to another, through the flow of time and tide, it still survives when 'four great empires' did not. At least the Needle is proud to say that – 'I was when London was not. / I am here'.

Even there are similar Egyptian sites and treasures in Istanbul, still, my students feel difficult to identify with the powerful images of human civilization which Cleopatra's Needle in London is representing, which is more than four thousand years old. The grand history of power struggle seems to be hard to imagine, when comparing to an emotion of a personal scale. The main emotion of the part (VII) from Tennyson's *In Memoriam* is grief – as the friend is gone, the house becomes 'dark', the street becomes 'long' and 'unlovely'. The heart 'used to beat so quickly', used to be excited, because the speaker's friend used to welcome him, with the hand of his friendship. Now, the friend is gone, he cannot sleep, as the house does not feel the same. Only the London street is alive, but it does not bring any pleasure, because it just means 'noise', and the tears of the speaker in 'the drizzling rain', because he does not know how the face another empty day, without his friend.

Arnold, the Poor, and the Spiritual Power

The spirit of a poet has an image of the burning flame, as E B Browning sees in the French writer George Sand, in a way which 'a poet-fire' is the 'burnest' 'large flame' (Browning 1083), making the heart of the poet beating 'purer', 'higher' (Browning 1083). The burning flame symbolises the poet's passion and desire for poetry. And yet, in one's ordinary everyday life, a burning fire could cause physical and psychological pain. Some students in the class have the experience of being burnt. Even they do not experience it, their family members may have it. Or, they have seen in the hospital, the Syrian children cried and screamed and died, because those children could not take the pain – the burning pain which even the strongest painkiller cannot work.

Although from a different religious background, my students have no difficulty to understand the situation of the poor, as they see in their daily lives. The homeless and the poor working class in Matthew Arnold's 'West London' and 'East London' come to depict the 'common human fate' (Ford 409), which requires a generous humanity to understand. Here are the two poems:

West London

Crouched on the pavement, close by Belgrave Square,
A tramp I saw, ill, moody, and tongue-tied.
A babe was in her arms, and at her side
A girl; their clothes were rags, their feet were bare.

Some labouring men, whose work lay somewhere there,
Passed opposite; she touched her girl, hied
Across, and begged, and came back satisfied.
The rich she had let pass with frozen stare.

Thought I: "Above her state this spirit towers;
She will not ask of aliens, but of friends,
Of sharers in a common human fate.

She turns from that cold succour, which attends
The unknown little from the unknowing great,
And points us to a better time than ours." (Ford 409).

East London

'Twas August, and the fierce sun overhead
  Smote on the squalid streets of Bethnal Green,
  And the pale weaver, through his windows seen
In Spitalfields, looked thrice dispirited;

I met a preacher there I knew, and said:
  "Ill and o'verworked, how fare you in this scene?"

"Bravely!" said he; "for I of late have been
Much cheered with thoughts of Christ, *the living bread*."

O human soul! as long as thou canst so
Set up a mark of everlasting light,
Above the howling senses' ebb and flow,

To cheer thee, and to right thee if thou roam,
Not with lost toil thou labourest through the night!
Thou mak'st the heaven thou hop'st indeed thy home (Ford 410).

In Arnold's two London poems, *East London* and *West London*, my students can easily identify themselves with the poor homeless woman (who does not belong to any kinds of social class) and the poor working-class 'pale weaver' (Ford 410), as they can see in their daily life, going to or coming back from school. The tramp's and the pale weaver's pain comes from another kind of suffering, although it is different from the kind of a burning pain. Both of them, although one in East London, the other is in the West, are 'ill' (Ford 409, 410). The poor woman is ill and moody, because she does not have a home. She and her children do not have enough food and clothes. That is why she is 'moody' and 'tongue-tied' (Ford 409). The pale weaver, on the other hand, is ill, because of he is 'o'erworked' (Ford 410). Too long working hours, and yet, it is still not enough for his and his family's survival.

The poet somehow reminds the reader, that only 'human soul' (Ford 410) can save us. Our soul can '[s]et up a mark of everlasting light' (Ford 410), which can reach beyond all seductions, all 'howling senses' ebb and flow' (Ford 410) – all coming and going of human desires, feelings, and illusions. Our soul can lift us to a state, which reminds us that we all share 'a common human fate' (Ford 409) – we were born, we grow, through aging, and we die. Although the future of the homeless poor woman in *West London* is unknown, the poet sincerely hopes that whenever she turns or asks to someone, it will be a turn 'to a better time than ours' (Ford 409).

Cityscape and Cultural Identity

In William Wordsworth's *Composed Upon Westminster Bridge, September 3, 1802*, the reader can see the way in which the poet depicts the view of the city with a sincere appreciation of its beauty:

Composed Upon Westminster Bridge, September 3, 1802

Earth has not anything to show more fair:
Dull would he be of soul who could pass by
A sight so touching in its majesty;
This City now doth, like a garment, wear
The beauty of the morning: silent, bare,
Ships, towers, domes, theatres, and temples lie

Open unto the fields, and to the sky;

All bright and glittering in the smokeless air.

Never did sun more beautifully steep

In his first splendour, valley, rock, or hill;

Ne'er saw I, never felt, a calm so deep!

The river glideth at his own sweet will:

Dear God! the very houses seem asleep;

And all that mighty heart is lying still!

In the city of London, in the early morning, the glory of the Sun comes to make an atmosphere of 'dreamy tranquillity' (Pater 3). For the poet, London has its majestic power, for its stunning view. London is 'beautiful', 'silent'. In the poet's eyes, the city is 'so touching in its majesty', with its 'ships, towers, domes, theatres, and temples', in a way which the poet's soul is in a deep feeling of calmness.

The poet's inner self, his soul, comes to identify with London, seeing the city as a representation of the essence of a majestic grace (nature, the Sun) and a cultural power (in different architectural forms), which touches and moves the poet's soul. The city of London here, is a great inspiration, which reinforces the poet's subjectivity, his individual consciousness, and his self-fulfilment. Among my students, very few of them, say, two out of seventy, had visited London. Even so, from another cultural, as Turkish, as my students are, can identify themselves with the poet's appreciation to the city's greatness – for London is not only the financial and political capital of England – it is, ultimately, the cultural capital and the home of creativity of the country. My students' feeling of being able to identify with another culture, such as the poet's 'English discourse' (Easthope 57), seeing the value and the significance of a different culture, is indeed, showing love and understanding in a sense of humanity. For me, I see this capacity of identifying with another culture as a way of expressing the strength of the self, the assurance of the self, in the grand existence of humanity.

Conclusion

To teach London poetry to English majors in Turkey has its own significant cultural meanings. The sense of Englishness, in the poems, comes as a Spring breeze, inspiring my students to think, to see, and to feel in another way. Nevertheless, through cultural identification, this Englishness somehow transforms, from so-called 'another' culture to mingle with my students' Turkish minds, giving birth to a new cultural identity, which goes beyond the dialectic of 'English' or 'Turkish'.

The cultural transformation in my London poetry class is a complex subjective process. It goes from a cultural community, to another one, comes back with a sense of self-realization, 'self-transformation' (Connor 217) and self-recognition. It gives the creative power to the renewal of life and emotion. Moreover, it gives a creative passion and desire, after the inner calmness and peace. With that, my students are much more able to see, to understand, even to enjoy their own condition of life.

Works Cited

Baldick, Chris. *Oxford Dictionary of Literary Terms*. Oxford: Oxford University Press, 2008.

Browning, E B. 'To George Sand: *A Recognition*'. *The Norton Anthology of English Literature: Volume 2*. Eds. Stephen Greenblatt and M. H. Abrams. New York: W. W. Norton, 2006.

Connor, Steven. 'What can Cultural Studies do'? *Interrogating Cultural Studies: Theory, Politics and Practice*. Ed. Paul Bowman. London: Pluto, 2003.

Easthope, Antony. *Englishness and National Culture*. London: Routledge, 1999.

Ford, Mark, ed. 'Introduction'. *London: A History in Verse*. Cambridge: MA, Harvard University Press, 2012.

Lin, Allison Tzu Yu. 'Teaching English and Cultural Exchange in Gaziantep'. *A Moment of Joy: Essays on Art, Writing and Life.* Taipei: Showwe, 2014.

Pater, Walter. *The Renaissance.* Oxford: Oxford University Press, 1998.

Woolf, Virginia. *The Common Reader II.* Ed. Andrew McNeillie. London: Vintage, 2003.

London Poetics

Chapter 5

Urbanity

This research aims to read John Keats's poetic style, in terms of the relation between solidity and sociability in the city of London. Keats's London poems show a specific urban style of his own, in a way which the dialectic of the self and the social relations is revealed in the representation of London. The inwardness of Keats's self and his domestic sphere in Hampstead come to claim a life style of leisure, rest, and recreation, while the social sphere of London, such as the Mermaid Tavern, comes to show the poet's other self in social terms. The inner and the outer worlds in Keats's poems construct the urbanity of his poetic style, as the dialectic of silence and activeness, calmness and social mobility comes to synthesise Keats's life and self.

Virginia Woolf, in her essay 'Great Men's Houses',

depicted John Keats's house in Hampstead, London. The place and the house itself are both showing something particular. Hampstead is not just a 'suburb'. It is 'a place with a character peculiar to itself', as if 'it is always spring in Hampstead' (Woolf, 'Great Men's Houses' 42). Keats's house, as one of the 'neat boxes' (Woolf, 'Great Men's Houses' 43) in Hampstead, has its particular style, 'as if designed for people of modest income and some leisure who seek rest and recreation' (Woolf, 'Great Men's Houses' 43). This specific character of Hampstead and Keats's house in it, somehow comes to form 'an urbanity in the style which proclaims the neighbourhood of a great city' (Woolf, 'Great Men's Houses' 43).

Keats's urbanity in his London poems reveals the dialectic of solidity and sociability, just as his house in Hampstead. As Keats quietly did his reading, writing and thinking in the house, 'died young and unknown and in exile' (Woolf, 'Great Men's Houses' 45), London and its life, as Virginia Woolf once depicted, goes on outside the window. [...]. Life goes on outside the

wooden paling. [...]. If we cross the road, taking care not to

be cut down by some rash driver – [...] – we shall find ourselves on top of the hill and beneath shall see the whole

of London lying below us. It is a view of perpetual fascination at all hours and in all seasons (Woolf, 'Great Men's Houses' 46).

The same sense of calmness, peace, and 'time out of mind' (Woolf, 'Great Men's Houses' 46) sentimental feeling is revealed in both the inner and the outer worlds of Keats's, as from the same hill (Parliament Hill), here comes the song of birds, London's 'dominant domes', guardian cathedrals', (Woolf, 'Great Men's Houses' 46), Keats, Coleridge, Shakespeare, and 'the usual young man sits on an iron bench clasping to his arms the usual young woman' (Woolf, 'Great Men's Houses' 47).

Inside of the window of Keats's little white house, the reader has an impression of 'clarity', 'dignity' and 'self-control' (Woolf, 'Great Men's Houses' 44) of Keats's short life, which shows 'the passion of love and its misery' (Woolf, 'Great Men's Houses' 44). And yet, outside of the window, 'life goes on' as 'the butcher delivering his meat from a small red motor van', 'some rush driver [...] they drive so fast [...] down these wide streets' (Woolf, 'Great Men's Houses' 46). As one stands on the top of the hill, one thinks about the contrast between aesthetics and materials. On the top of the hill, where one can see 'the whole of London', aesthetically speaking, the view of London is a representation of aesthetic emotion – 'a view of perpetual fascination at all hours in all seasons' (Woolf, 'Great Men's Houses' 46). On the other hand, materially speaking, when the 'usual' (Woolf, 'Great Men's Houses' 47) aspect of everyday life comes to one's own sight and one's own mind, including the concern of eating, drinking, crossing the road and using motor cars, one has to somehow look at London as a production

of human consciousness and 'its survival' (Dollimore 4),
particularly in some human conditions.

"To one who has been long in city pent"

To one who has been long in city pent
  'T is very sweet to look into the fair
  And open face of heaven, to breathe a prayer
Full in the smile of the blue firmament.
Who is more happy, when, with heart's content,
  Fatigued he sinks into some pleasant lair
  Of wavy grass and reads a debonair
And gentle tale of love and languishment?
Returning home at evening, with an ear
  Catching the notes of Philomel, an eye
Watching the sailing cloudlet's bright career,
  He mourns that day so soon has glided by,

E'en like the passage of an angel's tear
  That falls through the clear ether silently. (Ford 363)

In 'To one who has been long in city pent', the reader can see that the solitude speaker is happy, as the nightingale is 'too happy' in its 'happiness' (Keats 903), in its own singing. Yet, when the day ends 'so soon' (Ford 363), just like 'an angel's tear' drops 'silently' (Ford 363), I feel that this moment of reflection in the poem can be as 'immortal' and as 'intense' (Lin 411), as delicate as an aesthetic emotion, which makes one cry.

In the city of London, it is somehow 'very sweet to look into' the 'fair' (Ford 363) sky, with one's own 'heart's content' (Ford 363) and happiness. Being alone and feeling happy, one 'sinks into' the 'wavy grass' (Ford 363), reading 'gentle tale of love and languishment' (Ford 363). Coming home in the evening, one comes to hear the songs of the Philomel, looking at the cloud, which is 'bright' (Ford 363) because of the sunset. One's state of mind is happy and cheerful, which comes to synthesise the 'smile of the blue firmament' (Ford 363) and 'the notes' of nightingale (Ford 363) in London.

Lines on the Mermaid Tavern

Souls of Poets dead and gone,
What Elysium have ya known,
Happy field or mossy cavern,
Choicer than the Mermaid Tavern?
Have ye tippled drink more fine
Than mine host's Canary wine?
Or are fruits of Paradise
Sweeter than those dainty pies
Of venison? Oh, generous food,
Dressed as though bold Robin Hood
Would, with his Maid Marian,
Sup and bowse from horn and can.

I have heard that on a day
Mine host's sign-board flew away,
Nobody knew whither, till
An astrologer's old quill
To a sheepskin gave the story;
Said he saw you in your glory,
Underneath a new old sign
Sipping beverage divine,
And pledging with contented smack
The mermaid in the Zodiac.

Souls of Poets dead and gone,
What Elysium have ye known,
Happy field or mossy cavern,
Choicer than the Mermaid Tavern? (Ford 365)

The social sphere, such as a public drinking club house as the Mermaid Tavern itself, comes to show a sense of intense passion in Keats's sense. Even Ben Johnson and Shakespeare were long gone, as 'Souls of Poets dead and gone' (Ford 365), the place is still, in Keats's poem, representing the imaginary cityscape of the 'divine' and the 'glory' (Ford 365), highlighting the literary achievement of the great poets, as 'The Mermaid in the Zodiac' (Ford 365).

Anne Ridler
Wentworth Place: Keats Grove

The setting sun will always set me to rights …
    Keats, to Benjamin Bailey
Keats fancied that the nightingale was happy
Because it sang. So beautiful his garden,
Behind the gate that shuts the present out
With all its greed and grimy noise,
I fall into a like mistake, to think –
Because there are such depths of peace and greenness,

Greenness and peace, because the mulberry
Invites with arms supported like the prophet,
Because the chestnut candles glimmer crimson –
That heartache could not flourish among these flowers,
Nor anguish resist the whisper of the leaves.

Angry for him, blessing his gift, I accuse
The paradise that could not save him,
Sickness and grief that sunsets could not heal. (Ford 574)

Poetry, art, philosophy – these can somehow ease suffering, as 'no medicine can cure all diseases' (qtd. in Holstein 34). As Michael E. Holstein claims, pain can be described in poetry, in order to 'alleviate the sufferings of humanity' (Holstein 35). In Anne Ridler's poem, the reader can see that pain cannot be healed by nature ('sunsets could heal'), as pain can be read as a symbol of different things, such as 'a protest against social evils', 'desire for revenge', 'guilt and atonement' (Holstein 36), 'suffering in romance or romantic love' as Keats's 'relationship with Fanny Brawne' (Holstein 39 - 40) and so on, so forth. Writing about pain and suffering, in some ways, comes to demonstrate an act of 'humanitarian capacity' (Holstein 36), as Keats, Wordsworth, Coleridge, and Virginia Woolf, all did.

Works Cited

Dollimore, Jonathan. 'Introduction: Shakespeare, Cultural Materialism and the New Historicism'. *Political Shakespeare: Essays in Cultural Materialism.* Eds. Jonathan Dollimore and Alan Sinfield. Manchester: Manchester University Press, 1994.

Ford, Mark, ed. *London: A History in Verse.* Cambridge, MA: Harvard University Press, 2012.

Holstein, Michael E. 'Keats: The Poet-Healer and the Problem of Pain'. *Keats – Shelly Journal.* 36 (1987): 32 – 49.

Lin, Tzu Yu Allison. 'London in Love'. *Journal of Literature and Art Studies* 5.6 (2015): 408 – 411.

Keats, John. 'Ode to a Nightingale'. *The Norton Anthology of English Literature: Volume 2.* Eds. Stephen Greenblatt and M. H. Abrams. New York: W. W. Norton, 2006.

Woolf, Virginia. 'Great Men's Houses'. *The London Scene.* London: Snowbooks, 1975.

讀詩人94　PG1635

 London Poetics

作　　　者	林孜郁（Allison Tzu-Yu Lin）
責任編輯	洪仕翰
圖文排版	周政緯
封面設計	蔡瑋筠

出版策劃	釀出版
製作發行	秀威資訊科技股份有限公司
	114 台北市內湖區瑞光路76巷65號1樓
	電話：+886-2-2796-3638　傳真：+886-2-2796-1377
	服務信箱：service@showwe.com.tw
	http://www.showwe.com.tw
郵政劃撥	19563868　戶名：秀威資訊科技股份有限公司
展售門市	國家書店【松江門市】
	104 台北市中山區松江路209號1樓
	電話：+886-2-2518-0207　傳真：+886-2-2518-0778
網路訂購	秀威網路書店：http://www.bodbooks.com.tw
	國家網路書店：http://www.govbooks.com.tw
法律顧問	毛國樑　律師
總 經 銷	聯合發行股份有限公司
	231新北市新店區寶橋路235巷6弄6號4F
	電話：+886-2-2917-8022　傳真：+886-2-2915-6275

出版日期	2016年9月　BOD一版
定　　　價	200元

Printed in Taiwan

讀 者 回 函 卡

感謝您購買本書，為提升服務品質，請填妥以下資料，將讀者回函卡直接寄
回或傳真本公司，收到您的寶貴意見後，我們會收藏記錄及檢討，謝謝！
如您需要了解本公司最新出版書目、購書優惠或企劃活動，歡迎您上網查詢
或下載相關資料：http:// www.showwe.com.tw

您購買的書名：＿＿＿＿＿＿＿＿＿＿＿＿＿＿＿＿＿＿＿＿＿＿＿＿＿

出生日期：＿＿＿＿＿年＿＿＿＿＿月＿＿＿＿＿日

學歷：□高中 (含) 以下　　□大專　　□研究所 (含) 以上

職業：□製造業　□金融業　□資訊業　□軍警　□傳播業　□自由業
　　　□服務業　□公務員　□教職　　□學生　□家管　　□其它＿＿＿

購書地點：□網路書店　□實體書店　□書展　□郵購　□贈閱　□其他

您從何得知本書的消息？

　□網路書店　□實體書店　□網路搜尋　□電子報　□書訊　□雜誌
　□傳播媒體　□親友推薦　□網站推薦　□部落格　□其他＿＿＿＿＿

您對本書的評價：(請填代號　1.非常滿意　2.滿意　3.尚可　4.再改進)

　封面設計＿＿＿　版面編排＿＿＿　內容＿＿＿　文／譯筆＿＿＿　價格＿＿＿

讀完書後您覺得：

□很有收穫　□有收穫　□收穫不多　□沒收穫

對我們的建議：＿＿＿＿＿＿＿＿＿＿＿＿＿＿＿＿＿＿＿＿＿＿＿

＿＿＿＿＿＿＿＿＿＿＿＿＿＿＿＿＿＿＿＿＿＿＿＿＿＿＿＿＿＿＿

＿＿＿＿＿＿＿＿＿＿＿＿＿＿＿＿＿＿＿＿＿＿＿＿＿＿＿＿＿＿＿

＿＿＿＿＿＿＿＿＿＿＿＿＿＿＿＿＿＿＿＿＿＿＿＿＿＿＿＿＿＿＿

11466
台北市內湖區瑞光路 76 巷 65 號 1 樓

秀威資訊科技股份有限公司　　　收

BOD 數位出版事業部

....

（請沿線對折寄回，謝謝！）

姓　　名：＿＿＿＿＿＿＿＿＿　年齡：＿＿＿＿　性別：□女　□男

郵遞區號：□□□□□

地　　址：＿＿＿＿＿＿＿＿＿＿＿＿＿＿＿＿＿＿

聯絡電話：(日) ＿＿＿＿＿＿＿＿＿　(夜) ＿＿＿＿＿＿＿＿＿

E-mail：＿＿＿＿＿＿＿＿＿＿＿＿＿＿＿＿＿＿